The Seven

CHAIRS

HELEN LANTEIGNE

Illustrations by
MARYANN KOVALSKI

KPk
Key Porter Kids

Hey pumpkin, love Mom
—H.L.

For Gregory, Jenny, Joanna and Max
—M.K.

Canadian Cataloguing in Publication Data

Lanteigne, Helen, 1948-
  The seven chairs

ISBN 1-55013-959-2

I. Kovalski, Maryann. II. Title.

PS8573.A588S48 1998   jC813'.54   C98-930372-1
PZ7.L2915Se 1998

The publisher gratefully acknowledges the support of the Canada Council for the Arts and the Ontario Arts Council for its publishing program.

The Canada Council | Le Conseil des Arts
For the Arts | du Canada
since 1957 | depuis 1957

Key Porter kids
is an imprint of
Key Porter Books Limited
70 The Esplanade
Toronto, Ontario
Canada M5E 1R2

www.keyporter.com

Design: Peter Maher

Printed and bound in Italy

98 99 00 01 02 6 5 4 3 2 1

In his lifetime he made seven chairs.

The first chair, made
when he was a boy, was a
small three-legged stool.
It wobbled.

When it was done, he put
it in front of the hearth fire.

It became the property
of the calico cat.

The second chair had a back and two arms.
As he was a young man and very much in love,
he carved a heart into the chairback.

A fat lady bought the chair to sit in while having her portrait painted.

She leaned back heavily against the heart and splintered it.

But, of course, he never knew.

The third chair perched on perfect feet.
Being too poor to own proper woodworking tools,
he shaped each leg by hand.

Generations later, a London antique dealer
made a small fortune.

The fourth chair, perfect in detail and miniature in size, was made for his youngest daughter.

But the careless child lost it.

The tiny chair tumbled unnoticed to the earth and settled comfortably in the tall grass. Softly and slowly, it became part of the world around it.

The fifth chair landed in Paris. During a perilous sea voyage, the fifteen sailors were swept overboard and clung to the rungs and sides of the chair. Once safely ashore, they made a gift of the waterlogged chair to the nearest church.

This was a cathedral called Notre Dame, which is still to be found on an island in the middle of the river Seine.

Perhaps the chair is still there.

The sixth chair, his masterpiece, was done in the manner of Louis XVI at the request of a wealthy patron. Although it was intended as a gift to the Rajah, it eventually found its way to America, where it became the prop that held open the screen door of Miss Maybelle Jenkins's Beauty and Tea Parlor in South Maryville, Louisiana.

The town's ladies who sat on the soft chintz cushion
that Maybelle provided often remarked on the smooth
satin finish of the wood.

On a Tuesday afternoon one very hot July,
Mrs. Mildred Harkins was overcome by the heat
of the day and the fumes of her permanent wave.

While seated in the chair, she fainted.

After that Maybelle purchased paper Chinese fans for the ladies.

The seventh chair was finished when he was a very old man. It was a three-legged stool that wobbled.

He placed it beside the hearth.

It, too, became the property of the calico cat.